The Girl Who Could Fly

SOME OTHER BOOKS
BY WILLIAM H. HOOKS

Circle of Fire
The Legend of the White Doe
The Mighty Santa Fe
Snowbear Whittington
The Three Little Pigs and the Fox

The Girl Who Could Fly

By William H. Hooks
Illustrated by Kees de Kiefte

Macmillan Books for Young Readers • New York

Text copyright © 1995 by William H. Hooks
Illustrations copyright © 1995 by Kees de Kiefte

Macmillan Books for Young Readers
An imprint of Simon & Schuster Children's Publishing Division
Simon & Schuster Macmillan
1230 Avenue of the Americas
New York, New York 10020

Designed by Cathy Bobak
The text of this book is set in ITC Cheltenham Light.
The illustrations were done in pencil and ink.
Printed and bound in the United States of America
First edition
10 9 8 7 6 5 4 3 2 1

Library of Congress Cataloging-in-Publication Data
Hooks, William H.
The girl who could fly / William H. Hooks : illustrated by Kees de Kiefte .— 1st ed.
p.   cm.
Summary: Nine-year-old Adam doesn't want anything to do with the
new girl next door, but as he gets to know more about her and her
unusual abilities, they become best friends.
ISBN 0-02-744433-3
[1. Extraterrestrial beings— Fiction.   2. Friendship— Fiction.]
I. Kiefte, Kees de, ill.   II. Title.
PZ7.H7664Gi   1995
[Fic].— dc20   94-4582

For Nora Williams
— W. H. H.

Contents

Chapter 1

THE BALL

Her name was Tomasina. Her dad's name was Thomas. So I guess she was really Tomasina, Jr. But Tom was what she liked to be called.

Her mom's name was Ann, and their last name was Jones. Pretty ordinary, wouldn't you say? That's what I thought, too. That's what they wanted everybody to think.

The very first day the Jones family moved in next door to us, I met Tomasina. We bumped into each other in the hall. She said, "Hi, my name is Tomasina; what's yours?"

"Adam Lee," I told her.

"Any more Lees in the family besides you?" she asked.

"No," I said. "Lee is my middle name. There's more of us Grahams. But I'm the only one with a Lee."

"Oh," said Tomasina. "I see. Can I ask you a question?"

"Sure," I answered.

"Are you going to be my best friend?"

My mouth fell open and I just stared at her. Finally, I started to say that I already had a best friend.

"Thanks," she said. "I was hoping you would agree."

Then she wheeled around and went back into her apartment. I hadn't said a word about agreeing.

That best friend business was a little thing. Ordinarily I would have forgotten all about it. But the next day I ran into Tomasina on the street. She was whacking a ball against the sidewalk.

"Here, catch!" she yelled, and threw the ball to me.

I caught it, bounced it from hand to hand, and threw it back to her.

Just then, my mom called from our window. I looked up at her.

"Adam Lee!" she called again. "Get two quarts of milk. I'm making butterscotch pudding."

I turned toward Tomasina. The sun was in my eyes, but I could have sworn that the ball had stopped in midair. I blinked. The ball was still hanging in the air, not moving at all!

Tomasina snapped her fingers, and the ball dropped down. I reached out. It landed in my hands!

I squeezed the hard rubber ball. It was real.

Tomasina ran up to me.

"Did you see—?" I started to ask.

"Come on," she said. "I'll walk you to the deli."

Suddenly the ball felt hot. I handed it to Tomasina. She stuffed it into her pocket. I was itching to ask her where she'd gotten that trick ball.

"They don't have any more balls like this," she said. "They're all sold out."

For a moment I thought I *had* asked her about the ball out loud. But I hadn't.

"Hey, listen," she said. "If we're going to be best friends, you should call me Tom. Don't you think so?"

She was really starting to bug me. Who did she think she was? Pretty dumb, I thought. She didn't even know that going-on–ten-year-old boys don't have girls for "best friends." The guys at school would put her straight.

Buzz off, sister! That was what I ought to say to her.

"Hey, Adam," she said to me. "Does *buzz off* mean *okay*?"

"It means *get lost*," I yelled, and took off at a run for the deli.

I didn't look back. Just kept running. Fast. I was out of breath when I reached the deli.

I walked in. There was Tomasina, holding two quarts of milk. She handed them to me.

"What took you so long?" she asked.

Chapter 2

THE FRIDGE

For a couple of days, I didn't see Tomasina. Then she turned up at school. In my room.

The teacher did her usual bit. "This is Tomasina Jones, our new member. I want you all to welcome her to our class."

After that, Tomasina just seemed to melt into the woodwork. At lunchtime she disappeared. The same thing happened on the playground. But she was always at her desk when we came back to the room—so still and quiet, you could forget she was there.

I never saw her leave our apartment house to go to school. And we never walked home together. Thank goodness for that. I was afraid she'd be tagging along, especially after all that "best friends" business.

Then one day my luck ran out. I was walking home alone. I felt a tap on the shoulder. I turned. Tomasina.

"Mind if I walk home with you?" she asked.

I was still put out about our race to the deli. So I said, "I'll race you."

We took off. We were shoulder to shoulder for half a block. I noticed that Tomasina was puffing hard. I pulled out ahead of her.

This time I planned to look back and check on her. Every time I looked, I saw that she was falling farther behind.

When I reached the block our apartments were on, I checked again. She was almost a full block away. I cooled down to a walk. One of my sneaker laces was loose. I tied it, then jogged up the steps of our apartment house.

I opened the front door. There was Tomasina, standing in the hall! She was smiling.

I didn't know what to say. Weird, weird, weird! was all I could think.

"I pushed the elevator button already," she said.

The elevator door opened with a click. We got on. "Want to come in for a minute?" she asked.

It was the last thing I wanted to do. I don't know why I was saying, "Yeah, that would be nice."

She pulled out her key and opened the door.

The place was almost bare. There was a sofa and some chairs and tables. But it didn't look lived in. I thought maybe they hadn't unpacked all their stuff yet.

"Would you like some soda?" asked Tomasina.

"Yeah, I'm kind of dry," I said.

She went to the fridge and came back with a tall bottle of Coke and one glass.

"Is this okay?" she asked.

"Sure," I said.

She poured a glass and handed it to me.

"Aren't you going to have some?" I asked.

"Never drink," she said.

I thought that was a pretty strange answer. She hadn't said she never drank Coke. She'd said she never drank. I wondered what she meant.

"Would you like to see my maps?" she asked.

I swallowed a mouthful of Coke and started to answer. But Tomasina was out of the room before I could make a sound.

In a few seconds she was back with a huge black notebook. She plopped it onto the table. "Here are the maps I've been making," she said, opening the notebook.

My eyes bugged out. I wasn't the least bit interested in maps. But those were beautiful. They were works of art. I couldn't believe she had made them.

Page after page, one map was more beautiful than the next. The colors were like nothing I'd ever seen before. They were maps, all right. I could tell she was doing all the countries in South America. But they were more than maps. They had borders crammed with animals, birds, plants, and flowers.

The oceans around the countries looked like real water. Tiny waves seemed to roll up on the shores. There was so much squeezed into each map. It all looked alive.

I was so locked into the maps that I didn't understand what Tomasina was saying.

". . . Antarctica, the frozen continent at the South Pole," she said.

"What?" I asked.

"I was saying what I'm going to do next," she answered.

"What?" I asked again.

"Antarctica," she said. "I'm going to make a map of the South Pole."

My mouth was dry again. I took a big swig of Coke. "What are they for?" I asked.

"Ah, ah, ah," she said, waving a finger at me. "You're not to ask."

"They're beautiful. Why can't I ask?"

"That's a no-no. You can look only because you're my best friend. But even a best friend can't ask what my maps are for."

Slam! She closed the notebook right on my hand. Then she snatched it up and went to her room.

I polished off my Coke and started to leave. Then I remembered my manners. I took the empty glass and the Coke bottle back to the kitchen. I put the glass in the sink. I opened the fridge door to put the Coke back in.

There was nothing in the fridge. Well, almost nothing. Just a small platter with little cubes wrapped in silver foil. I picked one up. It was covered with strange markings that I couldn't read.

I heard Tomasina's footsteps. Quickly I put the cube back and closed the fridge door.

Tomasina was standing in the kitchen doorway. "Adam Lee," she said, "I've made a big mistake bringing you here. *Unless* you're really my best friend."

I mumbled something about being late and bolted out of the apartment.

Chapter 3
THE X-ORT

I thought about the maps all evening. I even dreamed about them that night. The tiny animals, birds, and flowers and those little waves really did move around in my dreams. It was like a cartoon happening on a map instead of a TV screen.

I wanted to talk to Tomasina about the maps. And about the strange cubes in the fridge, too. But she didn't ask to walk home with me the next day, or the next two days. Naturally, I couldn't ask her. What would the guys think? I'd be in for a lot of ribbing.

I was walking home by myself on Friday. Suddenly Tomasina appeared. I didn't hear her come up, but there she was, silent as a shadow.

I laughed. I always laugh when I'm nervous. "You want to know something?" I asked her.

"Yes," she answered.

"You're beginning to spook me."

"Does *spook* mean I make you laugh?" she asked.

"I don't get it," I told her. "I really don't get you, Tomasina—"

"I'd prefer Tom," she said.

"Well, Tom, let's get a few things straight. I want some answers from you."

"Like what?" she asked.

"Like, how did that ball hold still in the air? Like, how did you get ahead of me when you were way behind? Like, where did those weirdo maps come from? Like, why is there no food in your fridge? Like, how do you just appear out of nowhere? Like—"

"Hold it, Adam Lee!" she barked.

Then she seemed about to cry. I felt awful. But I was angry at her, too.

"I'm sorry," she said. "I've been testing you. Just a little bit at a time."

"What kind of grades am I getting?" I asked her.

"You don't get grades on this kind of testing."

"Well, what do you get?"

"You get accepted. Or you don't," she answered.

"Well, where do I stand?"

"So far, you're accepted," she said.

"What does that mean?"

"It means I can trust you. You've never told anyone—about the ball, the maps, or the fridge. Adam Lee, you are a best friend. Truly you are."

"How do you know I haven't told anyone?" I asked.

"Oh, I'd know right away if you did."

"How?"

"My x-ort would give a warning signal."

"Your what?"

"My x-ort. It's a little thing in the back of my head," she explained.

I shook my head. This was stranger than maps that moved.

"The next thing you'll be telling me is that you can fly," I said.

"I can," she answered.

"What do you use?" I asked, joking. "A broomstick?"

She just stared at me.

I felt itchy. "Are you some kind of junior witch?" I asked.

"Come on, lets go over to the park. We need a place where no one can hear us," she answered. "It's time I told you all about myself."

We headed for the park. But I wasn't sure I wanted to know all about Tomasina.

Chapter 4

THE OFF-BEATS

What Tomasina told me in the park really blew my mind. I figured I had three choices.

Choice number one: Forget it. Don't believe a word of what she said.

Choice number two: Believe it. Keep her secret a secret.

Choice number three: Believe it. Blow the whole thing. Tell Mom and Dad what was going on right next door to us.

That night I didn't just dream about Tomasina. I had nightmares.

Thank goodness the next day was Saturday. Time to join the Off-Beats at the youth center. That's our club. We meet every Saturday morning. Just guys. No girls allowed.

I left early for the center. No need to hang around and take chances on bumping into Tomasina.

Josh was there when I arrived. He was hanging out our sign, OFF-BEATS CLUB.

I gave Josh the secret "Off" hand signal. He answered with the secret "Beats" signal.

"What's up?" I asked.

"We've got to find a new member," Josh announced. "Lonny's dad has been transferred. They're moving to Texas."

"Wow, there goes our best pitcher. None of us can throw a ball like Lonny," I said.

Suddenly a picture flashed into my head: Tomasina pitching a ball that obeys her every command.

"Without Lonny, the Crushers will live up to their name. They'll crush us for sure," said Josh.

Other guys started coming in. Sammy, Leon, Carl, and Alex heard Josh's news. They all moaned together like a chorus. "We're lost without Lonny's pitching arm," Alex said.

It was the same with the rest of the club. As far as they were concerned, the Crushers had already won.

Finally Josh said, "That's enough! I'm calling for one minute of silence. Everybody, think. Think hard and come up with a new member. A new member with a great pitching arm."

Josh pulled out his stopwatch and said, "Silence starts now!"

We all closed our eyes.

I wished I'd kept mine open. As soon as my eyes were closed, I saw Tomasina.

She was pitching from the mound. A Crusher was at bat. Zap! Tomasina pitched. It looked like a strike. The Crusher at bat swung hard. But the ball curved just before it reached the batter.

"Strike one!" yelled the umpire.

The Crusher looked puzzled.

Zap! Tomasina pitched again. The same thing happened. The ball neatly curved over the bat. Another strike was called.

Tomasina wound up and pitched a third time. Repeat performance. The Crusher was out. The game was over. The Off-Beats won!

The crowd was yelling. "Tom! Tom! Tom with the magic arm!"

"Minute's up!" called Josh.

"Tom!" I yelled.

Everyone looked at me.

"Tom's the one who can do it," I said.

The words had just come out of my mouth. I felt as if I had no control. My mind was saying, *Stop!* What are you saying?

For a moment it was very quiet.

Josh said, "Who is this Tom?"

"A new neighbor of mine," I answered. "Someone who has a better way with a ball than Lonny," I added.

"Are you proposing this Tom for membership in the Off-Beats?" asked Josh.

"Yes," I gulped.

"Well, I hope he can do what you say he can," said Leon.

"He'll still have to pass the test to be an Off-Beat," reminded Josh.

"Yeah," said Carl. "He'll have to do something none of the rest of us can do."

"What's this Tom going to do?" asked Alex.

"I don't know," I told them. And I didn't. But I did know we'd all be in for a big surprise.

Chapter 5

COACH TOM

I walked home from the Off-Beats in a daze. What had I done? How could I get out of this one? What would Tomasina think? Worse, what would she do?

I needed time to puzzle it out. But no luck. There was Tomasina pounding that weirdo ball against the steps of our apartment house.

"Hi," I said to her.

"Hi," she answered, and kept on slamming the ball.

"I guess your x-ort was buzzing away this morning," I said.

She didn't answer, but just kept slamming the ball.

I was getting itchy again.

"I put a friend of mine up for membership in the Off-Beats club," I said. "I hope that was all right."

She stopped slamming the ball. But she still didn't say anything.

"What's the matter?" I asked. "Didn't your x-ort pick up what I said about you?"

"I got the message," she answered.

"Well?" I asked.

"Well, it bothers me," she said.

"What bothers you?"

"Let me get this straight," she said. "In your Earth sports, you always play fair. Right?"

"Sure," I said.

"Well, would it be fair if I pitched for you?" she asked.

I knew she had me there.

"But I've already told them you're the greatest pitcher. They're counting on you to save us from the Crushers! You've got to help us."

She started slamming the ball again.

I waited.

Finally she said, "Okay. Maybe there *is* a way I can help you."

"You mean you'll really pitch for the Off-Beats?"

"No," she said.

Then she threw the ball to me. "Come on," she said. "We've got work to do." She took off toward the park.

I followed. "Do you mind telling me what you're up to?" I asked.

"I'm up to turning you into the hottest pitcher in town," she said.

My heart sank.

Two hours later I thought my knees would sink. But not before my arm fell off. Tomasina had put me through such a workout that I was ready to drop.

"Enough!" she finally yelled.

I did drop.

She grabbed the ball and threw some tricky loop-the-loops. To an exhausted Earth person like me, it looked like magic.

"Let's jog home," she said.

I felt more like crawling.

"You show promise," she said, slapping me on the back.

I didn't feel like arguing.

"A month of practice like this every day. That'll do the trick," she said.

"What'll I tell the guys next week?" I asked.

"Tell them you'll pitch," she answered.

"But I promised to bring them this person named Tom with the great pitching arm."

"Okay," she said. "Tom will come along with you."

"But what are you going to do?" I asked. "New members have to do something no one else in the club can do. I thought you would do some fancy pitching tricks. What *will* you do?"

"I'll fly," she said.

Chapter 6

A DAY OF SURPRISES

The daily workouts with Tomasina were tough, so tough that I didn't think much about the flying business. Then Saturday morning arrived. It was time to bring Tom to the Off-Beats.

I thought about saying I was sick. If I could throw up, everyone would believe I was sick. I tried gagging over the sink. Nothing happened.

I fooled around, slowly getting dressed.

Mom called, "Adam Lee, there's someone at the door for you."

There was nothing left but to head out to certain doom.

Surprise number one greeted me: Tomasina—I mean Tom—looked very different. Her hair was hidden under a cap. She was wearing glasses with thick lenses. She was dressed in a sweatshirt, jogging pants, and sneakers. And strangest of all, she had freckles on her face!

"You think I'll pass?" she asked.

"Wow! Tom, you fooled Mom, and you almost fooled me! The guys will never know."

"It's the freckles that do it," she said.

I felt a little better. At least I wouldn't have to explain about bringing a girl to the club.

On the way there, I started to worry again.

"Turn off your worry button," said Tomasina. "This is going to be a piece of bread."

"I think you mean a piece of cake," I said.

I doubted it.

Second surprise of the day. The Off-Beats thought Tom was the greatest. They bought everything she said, hook, line, and sinker. Those guys were a bunch of pushovers.

"What you guys need is a good coach. That's me," she

told them. "And you need more than one super pitcher. You need a whole team that's good."

I could hardly believe what was happening. Tom was in charge. Right away she set up a practice schedule. She was running the whole show. And none of the Off-Beats seemed to notice. Or, if they did, they didn't care.

Finally Josh pulled out from under her spell.

"Wait a minute," he yelled. "Tom's not a member yet!"

"That's right," said Leon. "Tom has to do something none of us can do."

"What's it going to be, Tom?" asked Josh.

I held my breath.

"You're right, guys," said Tomasina. "And I'm ready for my membership test. Here's what we have to do."

Once again all the Off-Beats were caught in Tom's spell. She barked out orders. "No one but Off-Beat members can see what I do. Follow me!"

Tomasina marched out of the youth center. All of us Off-Beats followed her. On and on she marched, down to the waterfront.

I was thinking about that story of the Pied Piper. The one who led all the rats down to the river and drowned them.

When we came to a halt, we were standing on an old, deserted pier. No one else was in sight.

"This is a good place to take off," said Tomasina.

I rushed over and pulled her aside. "You sure you know what you're doing?" I whispered.

Tomasina fished something out of her pocket. It was one of those little cubes I'd seen in her fridge. She slipped off the wrapper and popped it into her mouth.

"Power cube down. Set to fly," she whispered to me.

Then she turned and faced the others. "Okay, guys, I'm going to fly," she said.

Some of the guys giggled. All of them looked puzzled.

Tomasina walked to the edge of the pier. She spread her feet apart and raised her arms. She began to shake.

I couldn't believe she was really going to do it. Even though she'd told me that day in the park that she and her mom and dad could fly.

Suddenly her sweatshirt and jogging pants began to fill out on the sides, like a balloon blowing up. From her wrists to her ankles, her clothes stretched out. She looked as if she were sprouting big webbed wings.

She tilted forward, right over the edge of the pier. Her feet

lifted off the ground. She rose quietly like a balloon. Then she wiggled her hands and glided out over the water.

She circled. She turned a loop-the-loop. She straightened up and sailed back toward the pier. There she hovered a few seconds, like a silent helicopter. Then, soft as a feather, she touched down on the pier.

No one made a sound. It was hard to believe what we had just seen.

Then the third surprise of the day struck. Words started coming out of my mouth. Words I hadn't planned to say.

"Well, guys, what do you think of that?" I said. "How

would you like to have a flight suit like Tom's? Pretty neat, huh?"

The guys still didn't say anything.

More words poured out of me. "Tom's dad is an inventor, you know. Always coming up with something new. That inflatable flight suit is his latest."

Thank goodness, I was getting her message loud and clear. The last thing I wanted was for the Off-Beats to find her out.

"This flight suit is still being tested," I added. "I know we can trust you guys to keep it secret."

The Off-Beats remained silent, most of them with their mouths hanging open.

"Is that a deal?" asked Tomasina. By then she was back to normal.

She stuck out her hand. The guys came up to her. They looked like zombies. Each one shook her hand. Each one promised to keep her secret.

Chapter 7

A PROMISE

During the next couple of weeks Tom whipped us Off-Beats into shape.

I surprised them with my pitching the first day. They didn't know I'd already had a warm-up week with Coach Tom.

At first I worried a lot about the flying business. But the strangest thing happened. Maybe I should say it didn't happen. No one said a word about flying. Either the Off-Beats were better at keeping secrets than I thought, or Tomasina had blocked the test from their minds.

Anyway, after two weeks I was feeling relaxed. And I was beginning to think we just might hold our own against the Crushers.

One day after practice Tom invited me to her apartment.

"I've finished my new map," she said. "Want to see what Antarctica looks like?"

"Isn't it just a huge pile of snow?" I asked.

"Come take a look," she said.

There was snow, all right—and more. Penguins and smaller birds dotted the shoreline. Whales and seals seemed to swim in the icy water.

This map was different. A misty layer covered most of it. But there was a hole in the mist. You could look through the hole and see all of the map clearly.

"What's this misty layer over the map?" I asked.

"Oh, that's the ozone layer," Tom answered.

"The what?" I asked.

"The ozone layer. It covers all of the planet Earth. It keeps the harmful rays of the sun out," she explained.

"But there's a hole in it," I said.

Tomasina laughed. "We came in through that hole," she

said. "We had flown by Earth many times before. We never saw any signs of life. On our last flyby we passed over Antarctica. Through the hole in the ozone layer we saw animals."

"And you came down for a look-see at the animals," I added.

"One animal led to another," she said. "From penguins and seals to humans. And finally to my best friend, Adam Lee."

Some of this she had told me that day in the park. But not about coming through the hole in the ozone.

I still didn't know how much to believe. Or how much not to believe. But after seeing her fly, I was believing more and more.

"Can I ask now what the maps are for?"

"Sure," she answered. "We're part of an intergalactic research team. Our job is to map the universe for signs of life. We hit a potjack here."

"I think you mean jackpot," I said. "Can I ask another question?"

"Sure," she replied.

"Where in the universe did you and your folks come from?"

Tomasina smiled. She shook her head and waved a finger in the air. "Sorry. That's a no-no," she said. "Besides, you couldn't send me a postcard there, anyway."

The postcard business made me feel uneasy.

"Does that mean you'll be leaving soon?" I asked.

"My last map is finished," she answered.

"But you can't," I said. "I'll miss you. What about the Crushers? We need you!"

She smiled. "I didn't say we were leaving today, or tomorrow."

I must have still looked doubtful.

"Don't worry," she said. "I won't leave until the Crushers are crushed. I promise."

Chapter 8

A SEALED SECRET

We took the Crushers by surprise. Without Lonny to pitch, they thought we would be pushovers. So they hadn't practiced much. They even laughed when I came up to pitch.

But not for long. It was three guys up and three guys out. Pitch. Swing. Miss! Tomasina couldn't have done it any faster than I did.

It was a short game. We smashed the Crushers twelve to nothing.

What a great feeling! The Off-Beats were usually the underdogs. Now we were the winners. And all of us knew it was because of Coach Tom.

We put Tom on our shoulders and marched around the field, chanting, "Our coach is red-hot!"

Tomasina looked a little puzzled when she heard the chant. I was afraid she'd ask what *red-hot* meant. But she didn't.

Finally Josh said, "Let's celebrate!"

Coach Tom yelled, "Follow me!"

We grabbed the sodas and corn chips we had brought. Then we ran to catch up with Tom.

It was the Pied Piper all over again. We followed Tom down to the river. The old pier was deserted, just as it had been the last time. Not a person was in sight.

We opened the soda and tore into the chips. Everyone was horsing around. Sammy spilled soda on Alex. Carl sneaked up and put crumbled chips down my sweatshirt.

Things were getting pretty wild.

Josh was standing at the very edge of the pier. He was waving his arms and yelling at us.

"Look, everybody," he called. "I'm going to fly!"

He tried to puff out his chest. He spread his feet apart and raised his arms. He began to shake, just the way Tomasina had done.

Everyone was laughing at his joke.

Suddenly he lost his balance. "Help!" he yelled. And down he went toward the water.

I knew Josh couldn't swim very well. And none of us had taken any lifesaving courses.

We all ran to the edge of the pier. No Josh anywhere. It was a long drop down to the water.

Then his head popped up. He was coughing and fighting the water with his arms. He went under again.

Some of the Off-Beats started yelling, "Help!"

Then we felt a rush of air over our heads. The next moment we saw Tomasina. She was in full flight over the river.

She swooped down and hovered close to the water.

Josh came up again.

Tomasina splashed into the river. She caught Josh under the arms and lifted him from the water.

I could see that she was straining. But she flew back up onto the pier, still holding Josh. She set him down gently.

We all crowded around Josh. He had swallowed a lot of water, but he was okay.

Suddenly Alex said, "Hey, guys, take a look at that."

He was pointing toward Tom.

At first I didn't know why he was pointing at her. Then it struck me. She had lost her cap rescuing Josh. The glasses were gone, too. Her hair was showing! She looked like a girl.

At that moment Tomasina raised her hand to her face. Water was dripping from her wet hair. When she brushed it from her face, she rubbed off her freckles.

This time no words came pouring out of my mouth to rescue her. I felt so helpless.

Tomasina motioned me to come near her. I walked over.

"My x-ort is picking up a message," she said. "I've got to get home right away." She turned and ran from the pier.

I knew I had to do something to seal the lips of the Off-Beats. I walked back to the group around Josh. "Off-Beats have their secrets," I said. "And Off-Beats keep their secrets."

I stretched out my hand and waited.

Josh was the first one to lay his hand on top of mine. "Secret sealed," he said.

One by one every Off-Beat placed his hand on top of mine and repeated, "Secret sealed."

We waited awhile for Josh to dry off. Then we left the pier. No one said a word. No one asked a single question about Coach Tom.

Chapter 9

A PIECE OF FOIL

I ran home, worrying all the way. Why had Tomasina left so suddenly? What was the message on her x-ort?

I took the elevator up to our floor. Then I went to her apartment. I was about to knock on the door.

Quietly, the door opened. Tomasina stepped into the hall. "Adam Lee, I'm sorry," she said.

"It's okay," I told her. "The guys won't tell anyone. They took the sealed-secret oath. It's okay."

"That's not what—"

I butted in before she could finish. "They think you're a hero. They'll never tell anyone," I explained.

"That's not what I'm sorry about," she said.

"No?" I asked.

"We're leaving," she whispered.

"When?" I whispered back.

"Right now," she said.

"Why?" I asked.

"Our mother ship is making a flyby over Antarctica. We've been ordered to board the ship tonight."

"Tonight!" I blurted out.

"Sh-sh, not so loud," said Tomasina. "I'll miss you, Adam Lee. I'll really miss my best Earth friend."

She dashed back into her apartment.

I stood in the hall, feeling awful.

I'm not sure how long I stayed there. I remember hearing a humming sound. Something like a motor warming up.

I reached out and pushed on the door. It moved. Tomasina had not locked it behind her.

I stepped into the apartment. The humming sound was very strong. It pounded in my ears.

Then I saw them. There were three windows in the living room. They were wide open. Tomasina was standing in the middle window. Her mom and dad were in the windows on each side of her.

They raised their arms. Wings began to grow from their wrists to their ankles. The three bodies tilted forward.

There was a great whooshing sound and a strong blast of air. They lifted off.

I ran to the window. I saw them join hands. They soared up and up, over the buildings.

I watched them until they were just tiny dots in the sky.

Then I blinked and they were gone.

I turned from the windows. Something caught my eye. A piece of shiny foil lay on the floor. I picked it up. It was the wrapping from one of their power cubes. It was under the middle window. And I was sure my best friend from somewhere-out-there had left it for me.

I often look at that little piece of shiny foil. And I wonder what the strange markings on it say. But best of all, it proves to me that I didn't dream the whole business about the girl who could fly.

ABOUT THE AUTHOR

WILLIAM H. HOOKS, former director of publications at Bank Street College, now devotes all of his time to writing. He is the author of over forty books for children. *The Three Little Pigs and the Fox*, illustrated by S. D. Schindler, was an ALA Notable Book, and *The Mighty Santa Fe*, illustrated by Angela Trotta Thomas, was described, in a *Publishers Weekly* starred review, as "triumphantly meshing the realistic and the magical." Mr. Hooks lives in Chapel Hill, North Carolina.